Ⴆ heeled Warriors is the story of the battle between the Lightning League and the Monster Minds. It is a valiant struggle of a brave band of friends who must defeat barbaric villains. The Lightning League's mission is to restore the Universe to its former state of peace, happiness and goodness.

CAST OF CHARACTERS

THE LIGHTNING LEAGUE
(The fighters for Good)

Jayce, *the leader*
Gillian, *a scientist*
Flora, *a plant-child*
Herc, *a space adventurer*
Oon, *a living suit of armor*

THE MONSTER MINDS
(The destroyers)

Saw Boss, *the tyrant*
Gun Grinner, *the enforcer*
Terror Tank, *the cannibal*
K.O. Kruiser, *the demolition expert*
Beast Walker and Launch Tank

THE LIGHTNING LEAGUE VEHICLES

Pride of the Skies—*the space barge*
Armed Force—*Jayce's favorite fighting vehicle*
Drill Sergeant—*specialty, drilling*
Quick Draw—*specialty, its hidden firepower*
Spike Trike—*specialty, digging and crushing*
Trail Blazer—*transport stalker*
Battle Base—*home base and control bridge*

WHEELED WARRIORS™

THE STALKERS STRIKE

A GOLDEN BOOK
Western Publishing Company, Inc.
Racine, Wisconsin 53404

Library of Congress Catalog Card Number: 85-070076
ISBN 0-932631-11-8
A B C D E F G H I J

There was a strange planet in darkest outer space. This world was always in shadow. Weird vines snaked away from the planet's surface and out into space. It was best to avoid this world. For it was the home base of beings who were trying to conquer the universe.

This was the domain of the Monster Minds—sinister thinking plants with powerful brains and fantastic powers.

In his throne room on that planet, Saw Boss, the master of all the Monster Minds, spoke to his subjects.

"If we are to spread across the universe," he said in his loudest voice, "we must go to more planets! We must drain them of their natural resources! We must grow more of our kind! We will strike again—now!"

As he spoke, he formed one of his tendrils into a fist.

3

Saw Boss' subjects, all plant beings, cheered.
Then, he led them outside. There, the dark energies
covering the planet made their plant bodies change.
Under these energies, each Monster Mind transformed
into a vehicle shape. Each one became a living, rolling
machine, armed with special powerful weapons.
"Follow me to victory," shouted Saw Boss.

Saw Boss shot an energy bolt at one of the vines. The vine, obeying Saw Boss, grew rapidly. It trailed off into space toward another faraway world.

Then Saw Boss led the other Monster Minds onto the vine. They all sped along the vine as if it were a growing freeway. Without friction to slow them down, the warriors moved at fantastic speed.

Meanwhile a huge space barge, the Pride of the Skies, sped through the same area of space. It was captained by an adventurer named Herc Stormsailor.

The ship was also the craft used by Jayce and the Lightning League. They were the only beings in the galaxy who dared to go up against the Monster Minds.

Inside the space barge were many scientific wonders.

Among the wonders was the Lightning League Battle Base, which was now the ship's control room. The Battle Base was one of many marvels invented by Gillian, a wizard-like scientist.

Gillian and his robot helpers were finishing their work on Trail Blazer. This was a big "Stalker" vehicle. It had many weapons and could travel over the roughest land. Trail Blazer could also be used in defense against the Monster Minds.

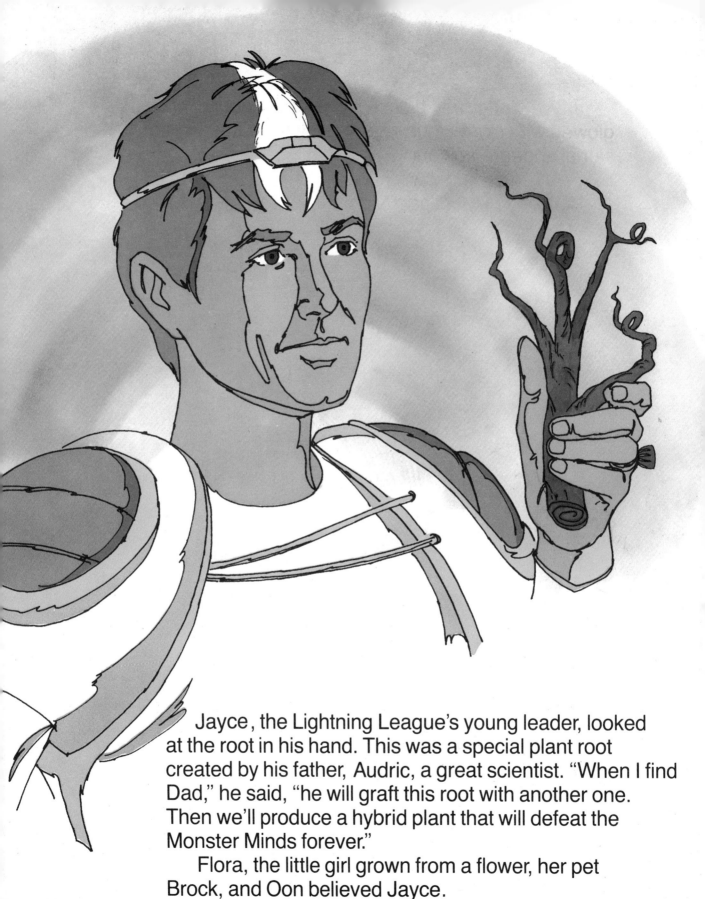

Jayce, the Lightning League's young leader, looked at the root in his hand. This was a special plant root created by his father, Audric, a great scientist. "When I find Dad," he said, "he will graft this root with another one. Then we'll produce a hybrid plant that will defeat the Monster Minds forever."

Flora, the little girl grown from a flower, her pet Brock, and Oon believed Jayce.

Jayce's ring, which once belonged to Audric, his father, glowed with mysterious energies. At the same moment, a signal appeared on one of the control panels.

"We're heading toward a planet, kid," Herc said to Jayce. "The planet doesn't appear on the space-map. Want to check it?"

Jayce nodded. "There might be a connection between the planet and my ring's glow. It could be Dad signaling us."

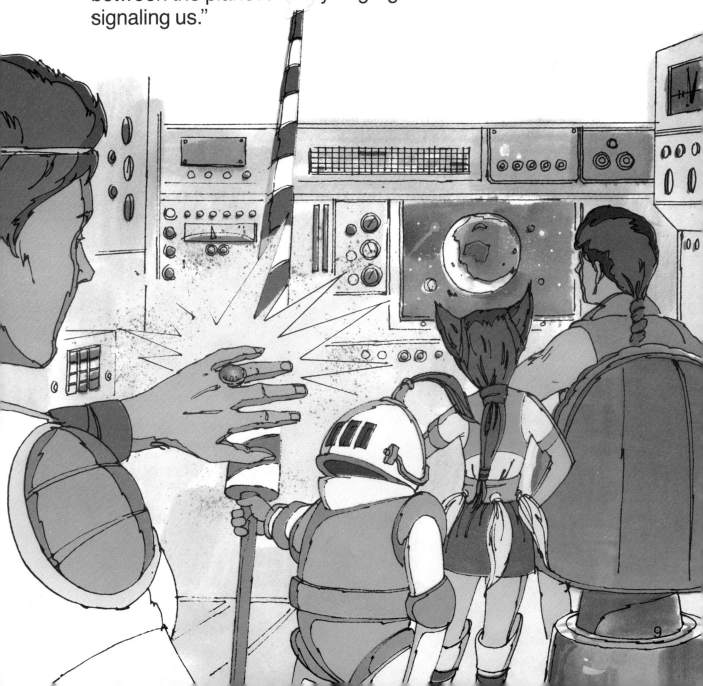

The Lightning League decided to land. Down below on the planet, people were going about their everyday work. These were simple farming people. They planted seed and harvested crops. Their tools were simple but good enough to get the job done. Every year their fields produced a good supply of food.

This world was rich in natural resources. It was a planet perfectly suited to the needs of the Monster Minds.

"This land now belongs to us!" growled a booming
voice. Then came the roar of mighty motors. Saw Boss
and his warriors had arrived.

    The Monster Minds called Terror Tank, Gun Grinner
and K.O. Kruiser rolled into view. Their faces twisted into
menacing grins.

    "These primitives can't stop us!" laughed Saw Boss.

But to the Monster Minds' amazement, the natives were more than they seemed to be. They knew just what to do— and they had the weapons to do it.

"They've got lasers!" yelled Gun Grinner in disbelief.

"Stop them!" shouted a farmer. "And capture their brains! Without their brains, they're just broken-down machines!"

The natives defended themselves like a small army.

"It's impossible!" shouted K.O. Kruiser. "Where'd they get those blasters? Who told 'em about our brains?"

"I'd eat those weapons," bragged Terror Tank, "if they'd just stop shooting them!"

"We need time to plan a better attack!" roared Saw Boss. "Retreat, warriors! Retreat!"

Saw Boss led his underlings into the woods.

The Pride of the Skies moved into orbit around the planet. Gillian then separated the Battle Base from the space barge. The Battle Base, with the Lightning League riding inside, lowered toward the planet's surface.

"Those anti-gravity beams of Gillian's sure come in handy," Herc said, "but they still make me a bit nervous."

The Battle Base gently landed.

Jayce and the Lightning League stepped out of the
Battle Base and into the new world. Gillian stayed
inside. He wanted to keep guard over the big vehicle.
  Flora, who was gifted with telepathic powers, felt
strange thoughts in her head.
  "What is it, Flora?" asked Jayce.
  "I sense other humans on this planet," Flora answered.

Jayce knew what that meant. Maybe his father was on this planet. He had to be sure.

Driving the mighty Stalker, Trail Blazer, Jayce led his small band. He took Armed Force, his favorite vehicle, along for the ride. Herc drove Drill Sergeant, Flora drove Spike Trike and Oon sat at the controls of Quick Draw. Jayce went off along rougher terrain, leaving his friends to go off in another direction.

"This reminds me of the time I battled the dragon lizard," boasted Oon. But his clattering armor proved he was not the bravest member of the Lightning League.

"Maybe you should have stayed behind," Herc told Flora.

But Flora's attention was someplace else. "The human thoughts are getting stronger," she said. "I'll try my best to lead us to them."

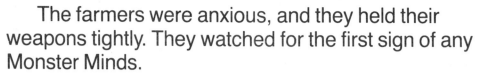

The farmers were anxious, and they held their weapons tightly. They watched for the first sign of any Monster Minds.

"Do you think the Monster Minds will come back?" asked one of them. "Will they make another attack?"

"I'd be surprised if they didn't!" said another native. "Remember what *he* told us. They never stop until they succeed."

18

The farmers kept on waiting.

Finally, they heard something powerful crashing through the underbrush. It sounded bigger than any of the Monster Minds.

Then the *thing* roared out of the woods! This was Beast Walker—the Monster Minds' own Stalker vehicle. It was heavily armed. And it had its own monstrous brain.

Again the farmers defended themselves. As before, they were brave. But this time, their weapons and courage were not enough.

"Puny humans!" roared Beast Walker. "Your weapons are like bees stinging a mountain! All you do is make me angry!"

Despite Beast Walker's threats, the farmers continued to defend their land. But they knew that the battle was lost.

In a short time, the battle was over. "Drop your weapons, humans!" Beast Walker ordered the defeated natives. They obeyed.

"You did splendidly," said Saw Boss. He rolled into sight with his three henchmen. "This land is now ours to do with as we please."

"And these weapons," grinned Terror Tank, "are mine! They'll make a tasty snack!"

"This planet's soil is perfect," said Saw Boss. He ran his wheels back and forth into the dirt. "Here we will plant seeds that will grow into more Monster Minds. The more we are, the more powerful we are."

One farmer whispered to the man next to him, "There must be someone who can help us. Anyone."

But there seemed to be no help at all.

Yet, help was on the way.

The signals in Flora's mind were getting stronger. She continued to drive Spike Trike closer to the source of those signals.

"Surprise, surprise!" mocked Herc, seeing the Monster Minds ahead. "If it isn't our old 'pals' again."

Beast Walker had already moved into hiding.

"Attack them!" commanded Saw Boss, starting his buzz saw.

K.O. Kruiser zoomed at Drill Sergeant. But Herc turned in time to avoid the full impact. Another fast move saved Herc and his vehicle from K.O. Kruiser's heavy wrecking ball.

Gun Grinner fired lasers toward Quick Draw. But Quick Draw had its own weapons. It fired them defensively toward Gun Grinner.

The Lightning League held their own against their foes.

Then Beast Walker rushed into the battle. "I will end this now!" he roared.

Beast Walker rose on its hind limbs. It towered over its foes like some giant from a nightmare. There was no way to avoid its powerful lasers. The battle quickly changed to the Stalker's favor.

"With Beast Walker," said Saw Boss, "nothing can beat us!"

When the dust settled, the three Lightning League members were prisoners of the Monster Minds.

"A battle well won!" Saw Boss said to Beast Walker.

"Not bad," said Terror Tank, "for a dumb Stalker."

"Careful what you say, metal-eater!" Beast Walker shouted. "Or I might forget we're on the same team."

Terror Tank rolled back. Even he feared the mighty Stalker.

"We have important matters
to discuss with our prisoners,"
said Saw Boss. "We must
learn *where* these primitives
got such modern weapons.
And we must find out *who* told
them about capturing our brains."
    "But what if the farmers
won't tell us?" asked
K.O. Kruiser.
    "Then we'll make them tell!"
said Gun Grinner.

In the meantime, Flora was busy. She knew that Jayce was the only person who could save them. She thought harder than she had ever thought before. She hoped to send Jayce a telepathic call for help.

Herc knew what Flora was doing, but he kept silent. He knew that the Monster Minds must not find out what she was trying to do. But Jayce was too far away for her to contact him.

However, Brock, the flying fish, was not too far away. He was able to get Flora's message. Brock, another of Gillian's creations, flew high and saw what was happening to his friends. Then, he soared off, looking around with his sharp eyes.

Brock flew over a large area. At last, he heard the sound of powerful engines. He followed the sound. Down below he could see Trail Blazer.

Flapping his wings fast, Brock got Jayce's attention.

"Where's Flora?" asked Jayce. "And where are the others? Did they find the humans of this world?"

Brock could not talk. Only Flora could understand the whistling sounds that he made. Even though Jayce could not actually understand Brock, he knew that something was wrong. He followed Brock into the woods with Trail Blazer.

The natives, meanwhile, realized that keeping silent would only make things worse. One stepped forward. He hoped that by talking he would save his people.

"Some time ago," he said, "a stranger came down to us from the stars. He flew a strange craft and was dressed as a beggar. He gave us our weapons and told us about your brains."

"That had to be Audric!" growled Saw Boss.

"Audric!" said Jayce. Trail Blazer's microphones had picked up Saw Boss' words. "My father *was* here! Could he still be here?"

He gunned the Stalker's engine, pushing it ahead at top speed.

Saw Boss and the other Monster Minds reacted with anger. Trail Blazer thundered toward them. Flora smiled.

"Beast Walker!" commanded Saw Boss. "Stop him!"

The monstrous Beast Walker sped toward Trail Blazer. Jayce was surprised. He had not expected the Monster Minds to have a Stalker too. In that moment of surprise, Jayce was distracted, and Beast Walker made his sudden attack!

His pincer claws grabbed Trail Blazer's hull. His super-strong front legs delivered the first blows. But Trail Blazer was only stunned.

The battle was just starting. Beast Walker's lasers were met by Trail Blazer's. The ground shook under the Stalkers' weight.

"Maybe you do have a Monster Mind brain," Jayce said to Beast Walker, "but my human brain puts me ahead in this game!"

Jayce then proved his point. Using Trail Blazer's might and some leverage, he raised the Stalker on its back legs and struck his giant foe.

Jayce fought fairly, but the same could not be said of the Monster Minds. When Jayce's attention was on the enemy Stalker, the other Monster Minds launched a sneak attack.

They attacked from behind, using all of their weapons. The air was streaked by countless powerful rays.

Trail Blazer was weakening under the Monster Minds' attack. There was little left for Jayce to do.

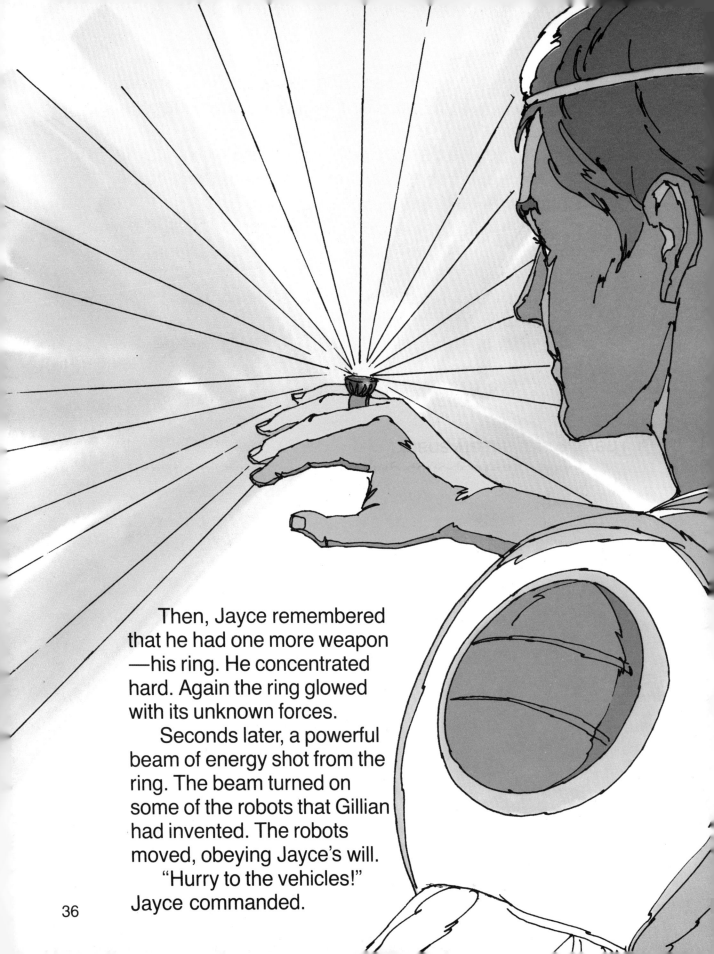

Then, Jayce remembered that he had one more weapon—his ring. He concentrated hard. Again the ring glowed with its unknown forces.

Seconds later, a powerful beam of energy shot from the ring. The beam turned on some of the robots that Gillian had invented. The robots moved, obeying Jayce's will.

"Hurry to the vehicles!" Jayce commanded.

Ducking the Monster Minds' lasers, each mechanical creature climbed aboard a different vehicle. Engines began to roar and wheels rolled.

"Stop those robots!" ordered Saw Boss.

But there was no stopping Armed Force, Quick Draw, Drill Sergeant and Spike Trike. The robots drove them toward the Monster Minds. The battle raged and the Monster Minds were losing.

Seeing his warriors beaten, Saw Boss again shouted his most hated word, "Retreat!"

"I'm not finished yet!" growled Beast Walker. He kept up his attack on Trail Blazer.

"You're finished now," said Jayce. Trail Blazer shot another defensive blast. The ray zapped in front of Beast Walker and disconnected part of his monstrous brain.

Beast Walker whined down to a stop. The battle was over.

"We'll repair Beast Walker on our own planet," said Saw Boss. He got the Stalker's engine running enough to get back home. Then Saw Boss led his warriors back to the vines that led out into space.

"They'll never come back here," said Jayce.

"Good work, kid," said Herc. He smiled at Jayce.

"I just wish we'd found Dad here," said Jayce. "At least he helped these people. And we know we're on the right track."

"I am certain you will find Audric someday," said Gillian. His voice was soothing and confident.

"Now that these people are safe," said Oon, "can we go back to the ship?"

Again, the Lightning League got inside the Battle Base. It lifted off to join the orbiting space barge.

"Someday we *will* defeat the Monster Minds," said Jayce.

Herc Stormsailor, Gillian, Flora and Oon walked up to Jayce. They smiled in agreement. Then, together, they said the motto of the Lightning League:

"'*A Courageous Heart, A Righteous Quest!*'"

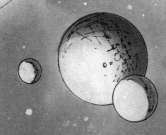